This Little Tiger book belongs to:

____

____

____

LITTLE TIGER PRESS LTD,
an imprint of the Little Tiger Group
1 Coda Studios, 189 Munster Road, London SW6 6AW
Imported into the EEA by Penguin Random House Ireland,
Morrison Chambers, 32 Nassau Street, Dublin D02 YH68
www.littletiger.co.uk

First published in Great Britain 2018
This edition published 2019

Visit Jane Chapman at www.janekchapman.com

A CIP catalogue record for this book is available from the British Library

 • ISBN 978-1-84869-934-2
Printed in China • LTP/2700/4248/1221
2 4 6 8 10 9 7 5 3

To Susan Beatson with grateful thanks
~ J C

Just Like You!

Jane Chapman

LITTLE TIGER
LONDON

Piccolo was the tiniest, fuzziest mammoth in the herd.
"Sweeter than honey," murmured Mama.
"Brighter than the brightest star," smiled Pops.
And they snuggled her cosily.

Piccolo soon began to wonder at the huge world around her.

"Wow," she gasped, as the mammoth herd travelled through vast icy plains and past towering icebergs.

She sheltered between Mama and Pops when storms raged, the sky's angry roars echoing through the mountains.

"You're safe with me, precious," whispered Pops, drawing her close. But Piccolo was afraid.

"I'm so tiny, and the world is **enormous,"** she thought. "When will I be big like Pops and Mama?"

Pops was Piccolo's hero.
He **toppled** the tallest trees so that
she could nibble on juicy shoots.

He **ploughed** through snowdrifts so that she had room to play.

He even snuffled up snowflakes
and puffed them out
in a cooling whoosh of sparkles!

But when Piccolo pushed at the trees, their leaves barely rustled.

When she tried to break through snowdrifts, she needed to be rescued.

And snuffling up snow always ended the same way.

AAAAAACHOOO!

"You light up my day, little one," laughed Pops, ruffling her fur.

"But I don't want to be little," sniffed Piccolo. "I want to be big and strong like you!"

"You will be one day – maybe even bigger," said Pops, "but for now, Mama and I are here to look out for you."

Piccolo sighed.

One day Pops had an idea.
"There's something special I'd like to show you, but it's a long way away," he smiled. "Do you feel big enough for a journey? Just the two of us?"
Piccolo squealed with delight.
"An adventure?!"

The next morning they waved goodbye to Mama and set off towards the mountains.

"Come on, Pops!"
Piccolo called.
"Try and keep up!"

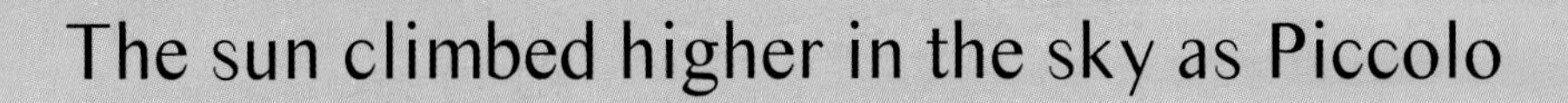

The sun climbed higher in the sky as Piccolo

hopped and jumped

in Pops's big footprints.

But her skipping turned to
shuffling as the day went on.

Slower . . .

and slower . . .

“Up you come, sweetheart,” chuckled Pops, scooping Piccolo high with his trunk and turning her around.

“I don’t want to go back! I want to keep going,” cried Piccolo. “What about the special something?”

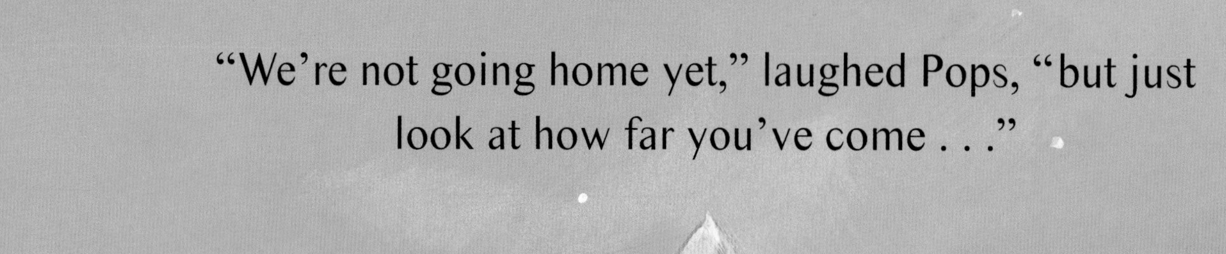

"We're not going home yet," laughed Pops, "but just look at how far you've come . . ."

Snaking away towards the horizon was a trail of footprints.

"I'm so proud of you," grinned Pops. "That is a very long walk for a very small mammoth."

Piccolo was amazed that her tiny steps had taken her so far.

Pops trudged onward until the low
sun turned the snow pink.

Rising up before them
was a **huge** tree,
leafless and alone.

"We're here," whispered Pops.
Piccolo was confused.
"But I thought we were coming
to see something special!"
she snuffled.

Pops slid Piccolo down his trunk.
"Look closer," he smiled.
There on the tree were lines and
swirls etched into the bark.

"Every mark celebrates a
mammoth," said Pops.
"Look, this is me! My mama
measured me up against this
tree when I was just the
same age as you."

"But you were **even smaller**
than me!" gasped Piccolo, tracing
the line with her trunk.

Pops took a stick and marked
just above Piccolo's head.
"Every year we'll come back
to this tree and you'll see that
you've grown a little
bit more," he said.

"And every year, you'll see
that you are still enormous,
Daddy!" giggled Piccolo,
scrambling up to make
him a new mark.

“Let’s go and tell Mama all about our day,” said Pops, turning into the wind. Snow whirled around his feet as they began the long journey home.

“I love you, Pops,” yawned Piccolo, snuggling into his soft fur. “And one day I’ll be big and strong, just like you!”